'No, n

your

it, I've got to
die . . . you
promised me . . .
you told me . . .'

IVAN TURGENEV
Born 1818, Oryol, Russia
Died 1883, Bougival, France

*Kasyan from the Beautiful Lands* is taken from
Richard Freeborn's first translation of *Sketches from a
Hunter's Album*, first published in 1967.

*District Doctor* is taken from Richard Freeborn's
second translation of *Sketches from a Hunter's Album*, 1990.

IVAN TURGENEV IN PENGUIN CLASSICS
*Fathers and Sons*
*First Love*
*Home of the Gentry*
*On the Eve*
*Rudin*
*Sketches from a Hunter's Album*
*Spring Torrents*
*Three Sketches from a Hunter's Album*

# IVAN TURGENEV

## *Kasyan from the Beautiful Lands*

*Translated by*
Richard Freeborn

PENGUIN BOOKS

PENGUIN CLASSICS

Published by the Penguin Group
Penguin Books Ltd, 80 Strand, London WC2R 0RL, England
Penguin Group (USA) Inc., 375 Hudson Street, New York, New York 10014, USA
Penguin Group (Canada), 90 Eglinton Avenue East, Suite 700, Toronto, Ontario,
Canada M4P 2Y3 (a division of Pearson Penguin Canada Inc.)
Penguin Ireland, 25 St Stephen's Green, Dublin 2, Ireland
(a division of Penguin Books Ltd)
Penguin Group (Australia), 707 Collins Street, Melbourne, Victoria 3008, Australia
(a division of Pearson Australia Group Pty Ltd)
Penguin Books India Pvt Ltd, 11 Community Centre, Panchsheel Park,
New Delhi – 110 017, India
Penguin Group (NZ), 67 Apollo Drive, Rosedale, Auckland 0632, New Zealand
(a division of Pearson New Zealand Ltd)
Penguin Books (South Africa) (Pty) Ltd, Block D, Rosebank Office Park,
181 Jan Smuts Avenue, Parktown North, Gauteng 2193, South Africa

Penguin Books Ltd, Registered Offices: 80 Strand, London WC2R 0RL, England

www.penguin.com

This selection published in Penguin Classics 2015
001

Translation copyright © Richard Freeborn, 1967, 1990

The moral right of the translator has been asserted

Set in 10/14.5 pt Baskerville 10 Pro
Typeset by Jouve (UK), Milton Keynes
Printed in Great Britain by Clays Ltd, St Ives plc

A CIP catalogue record for this book is available from the British Library

ISBN: 978–0–141–39871–6

www.greenpenguin.co.uk

# Contents

## District Doctor

One time in the autumn, on coming back from a long trip, I caught a cold and had to go to bed. Luckily the fever struck me in a provincial town, in a hotel, and I sent for a doctor. In half an hour the district doctor appeared, a man of small stature, thinnish and black-haired. He wrote out the usual prescription for something to make me sweat, ordered the application of a mustard plaster and very skilfully slipped his five-rouble payment into his coat cuff, all the while drily coughing and glancing to one side, and was just on the point of leaving when a conversation was struck up and he remained. The fever tormented me. I foresaw a sleepless night and was glad to chatter with the good fellow. Tea was served. My good doctor started talking. He was no fool and expressed himself vivaciously and rather entertainingly. Strange things happen on this earth: you can live a long while with someone and be on the friendliest of terms, and yet you'll never once talk openly with him, from the depths of your soul; while with someone else you may scarcely have met, at one glance, whether you to him or he to you, just as in a confessional, you'll blurt out the story of your life. I don't know what made me deserve the confidence of my new friend, save that, on the spur of the moment, he 'took to me', as they say, and recounted to me a fairly remarkable episode, and it is his story I now wish to relate to the well-disposed reader. I will try to express myself in the doctor's own words.

'You don't happen to know, do you,' he began in a weak and quavering voice (the result of unadulterated birch snuff), 'you don't happen to know the local judge, Mylov, Pavel Lukich? . . . You don't? . . . Well, it doesn't matter.' (He coughed and wiped his eyes.) 'So you see it was like this, as you might say, so as not to tell a lie – during Lent, just when everything was thawing. I was sitting with him, at our judge's house, and I was playing whist. Our judge was a good chap and very fond of playing whist. Suddenly' (my doctor friend frequently used the word 'suddenly') 'they tell me someone's asking for me. I ask what he wants.

He's brought a note – it must be from a patient. Let me see it, I say. Yes, it's from a patient . . . Well, that's all right, it's our bread and butter, you know . . . It's like this: the note's from a lady, a landowner and widow, who says her daughter's dying, come for God's sake, horses've been sent to fetch you. Well, that's not so bad so far, except that she's twenty miles away and it's dark outside and the roads are bloody awful! What's more, she herself's poorly off, there's no more'n couple of silver coins in it for me, and that's doubtful, probably I'll have to make do with a bit of cloth and a few crumbs of this and that. But duty comes first, you know, when someone's dying. Suddenly I transfer my cards to an inveterate member of our group, Kalliopin, and set off home. I see a little cart standing by my porch harnessed with peasant horses – big-bellied, huge-bellied, and woolly coats on 'em thick as felt – and a coachman's sitting there without his hat, as a mark of respect. Well, I think, it's clear as daylight, my good fellow, that your lords and masters don't eat off gold plate . . . You may laugh at that, but I'll tell you one thing, those of us who're poor, we notice these things . . . If a coachman sits there like a prince, for instance, and doesn't take his

3

cap off and even grins to himself under his beard and twirls his whip, you can bet you'll get a couple of real big banknotes! But I see there's not a whiff of that in this case. However, I tell myself, you can't do a thing about it – duty comes first. I grab hold of the most obvious medicines and set off. Believe it or not, I scarcely manage to get there. The road's absolutely hellish – streams, snow, mud, gullies, and then suddenly it turns out a dam's burst – one disaster after another! Still, I get there. The house is small, with a straw roof. There's light in the windows, meaning that they're waiting. I go in. I'm met by an old woman, very dignified, in a bonnet. "Please help," she says, "she's dying." I tell her: "Don't worry. Where's the patient?" "This way please." I find myself in a small, clean room, with a lamp burning in the corner and a girl of about twenty lying on the bed unconscious. She's literally blazing hot and breathing heavily in a fever. There are two other girls there, her sisters, frightened and tearful. "Yesterday evening," they tell me, "she was in perfect health and had a hearty appetite. This morning she complained of having a headache, but towards evening she suddenly became like this . . ." I tell them again: "Don't worry" – a doctor's obligation, you know – and I set to work. I bled her, ordered mustard plasters to be applied and wrote out a prescription. Meantime I'm looking at her, can't take my eyes off her, you know – well, my God, I've never seen such a face before – in a word, she's beautiful! Pity for her literally tears me apart. Such delightful features, such eyes . . . Then, thank God, she got a bit better, started sweating and realized where she was, looked around her, smiled, ran her hand across her face . . . Her sisters bent over her and asked her how she was. "All right," she says and turns over. I see she's gone to sleep. Well, I say, we must let her rest now. So we all go out of the room on tiptoe. Only a maid remains behind to watch over her. In the sitting-room the samovar's ready, along with a bottle of Jamaican – in my business, you know, you can't get by without a tot of rum. They offer me some tea and beg me to stay overnight. I say yes – after all, where could I go at that time of night? The old woman goes on groaning and sighing. "What for?" I ask. "She'll live, don't you worry. It'd be better if you got some rest yourself. It's two o'clock in the morning." "You'll be sure and rouse me if anything happens?" "I'll do that, I'll do that." The old lady went off to her room and the sisters went off to theirs. A bed was set up for me in the sitting-room. So I lay down, but I couldn't sleep. Hardly surprising, though you'd have thought I'd be worn out. I simply couldn't get the sick girl off my mind. Finally I couldn't stand it any more and suddenly got up, thinking I'd go and see what was happening to my patient. Her bedroom was just off the sitting-room. Well, I rose and opened her door softly, my heart beating like mad. I see the maid's asleep, her mouth wide open and snoring, the wretch! But the sick girl's lying with her face towards me and moving her arms about, poor thing. I'd no sooner approached than she suddenly opens her eyes and stares at me. "Who is it? Who's there?" I got confused. "All right, don't be frightened, my dear," I say. "I'm the doctor and I've come to see how you are." "You're the doctor?" "Yes. Your mother sent into the town for me. I've bled you, my dear, and now you must rest and in a couple of days, God grant, we'll have you on your feet again." "Oh, yes, doctor, you mustn't let me die . . . please, please." "Don't say such things, God be with you!" But her fever'd returned, I thought. I felt her pulse and found her feverish. She looked at me and then suddenly seized me by the hand. "I'll tell you why I don't want to die,

I'll tell you, I'll tell you . . . now we're alone. Only, please, don't tell anyone else. Just listen." I bent down to her and she strained her lips toward my ear and her hair touched my cheek – I can tell you, my head was spinning from being so close to her – and she started whispering . . . I couldn't understand a word . . . Of course, she was delirious . . . She went on whispering and whispering, so fast it didn't sound like Russian, and then she stopped, shuddered, dropped her head on the pillow and shook her finger at me. "See you don't tell anyone, doctor." I calmed her somehow or other, gave her a drink, roused the maid and left.'

At this point, sighing bitterly once again, the district doctor took some snuff and paused for a moment.

'However,' he went on, 'the next day the sick girl, contrary to my expectations, was no better. I thought and thought about her and suddenly decided to stay, although other patients were waiting for me . . . And, you know, you mustn't neglect your patients: a practice can suffer from that sort of thing. But, in the first place, the sick girl was in a desperate state; and, secondly, to tell the truth, I had a strong personal attachment to her. What's more, I liked the whole family. Although

7

they didn't have much in the way of possessions, they were extraordinarily well educated, one might say. Their father'd been a man of learning, a writer. He'd died, of course, in poverty, but he'd succeeded in giving his children an excellent education and he'd also left many books behind. Because I looked after the sick girl so zealously, or for some other reason, I have to say that they grew very fond of me in that household and treated me as one of the family . . . Meantime, the state of the roads became frightful. All communications, so to speak, were completely severed. Even medicine was only obtainable from the town with difficulty . . . The sick girl didn't get any better . . . Day after day, day after day . . . Well, you see, sir, you see . . .' (The doctor fell silent.) '. . . I don't rightly know how to put it, sir . . .' (He again took some snuff, wheezed and drank some tea.) 'I'll tell you straight out, my sick patient . . . how can I put it? . . . well, fell in love with me . . . or no, she didn't so much fall in love as . . . well, besides . . . I can't rightly say, sir . . .' (The doctor hung his head and went red.)

'No,' he went on vivaciously, 'it wasn't love! When all's said and done, you've got to know your own worth. She was an educated girl, intelligent, well-read, while I'd completely forgotten, one might say, all the Latin I'd ever learned. As for my figure' (the doctor glanced at himself with a smile) 'I didn't have all that much to boast about. But the Lord God hadn't made a complete fool out of me – I can tell black from white, you know, and I can make sense of things as well. For instance, I understood very well that Alexandra Andreyevna – she was called Alexandra Andreyevna – felt for me not love so much as what might be called a friendly disposition and a kind of respect. Although she may perhaps have been mistaken in her attitude, her state was, well, you can judge for yourself . . . Besides,' added the doctor, who'd spoken so brokenly and scarcely without drawing breath, in evident confusion, 'I've probably let my tongue run away with me, so you won't understand a thing . . . So, look, if you don't mind, I'll tell it all just as it happened.'

He finished his glass of tea and started speaking in a quieter voice.

'So it was like this. My patient grew worse – worse and worse. You're not a medical man, my good sir, so you can't understand what happens in the soul of someone like me, particularly at the beginning, when he starts to realize that the illness is getting the better of him. Your self-confidence flies out the window! You suddenly feel so small it's hard to describe. It seems to you you've forgotten everything you've ever learned, and your patient no longer trusts you, and others round you start noticing you're at a loss and start telling you the symptoms and looking at you from under their brows and whispering . . . oh, it's bloody awful! Surely, you think, there's got to be a medicine for this illness, it's just a case of finding it. Is this it? You try it – no, it's not that! You don't give the medicine time to work but try another, then another. You pick up your book of prescriptions and study it – ah, that's the one! Sometimes you just open the book at random and think, what the hell . . . But all the time the patient's dying, while another doctor might've saved him. You say you need a second opinion, because you can't take all the responsibility on yourself. And what a fool you look in such circumstances! Well, as time goes by you get used to it, it's nothing. Your patient's died, but it's not your fault, you followed the rules. But what's much worse is when you can see the blind trust they place in you, yet you feel you're not in any position to help. It was precisely such trust that Alexandra Andreyevna's family placed in me, while forgetting that their daughter was in danger. I was also, for my own part, assuring them it was all right, while my heart was right down in my boots. To cap all my misfortunes, the weather got so bad that the coachman couldn't go for the medicines for whole days at a time. And I never left the sick girl's room, couldn't tear myself away, told her silly jokes and played cards with her. At nights I sat beside her bed. The old lady thanked me with tears in her eyes and I thought to myself: "I don't deserve your thanks." I confess to you quite openly – there's nothing left to hide now – I fell in love with my patient. And Alexandra Andreyevna grew very fond of me and wouldn't allow anyone else into her room. She began talking to me, asking me where I'd done my training, what my life was like, who my parents were, who'd I go visiting? I felt I shouldn't let her talk, but I couldn't really stop her, definitely stop her, you know. I'd seize myself by the head and tell myself, "What're you doing, you blackguard?" But she'd take my hand and hold it, look at me, gaze at me, gaze and gaze at me and turn away and sigh and say, "How good you are!" Her hands were so hot, her eyes so round and longing. She'd say: "Yes, you're good, you're a good man, you're not like our neighbours . . . No, you're not like them at all, not at all . . . How is it we haven't met before?" And I'd say: "Alexandra Andreyevna, don't fret . . . Believe me, I don't feel, I've no idea why I should deserve this, only just don't fret, for God's sake, don't fret . . . everything'll be all right, you'll get well." But I ought to tell you, by the way,' the doctor added, bending forward and raising his eyebrows, 'that they didn't have much to do with the neighbours, because the small fry weren't really up to them and they were too proud to curry favour with the rich. I'm telling you they were an extremely well-educated family, so for me, you know, it was a privilege to be there. She'd only accept medicine from me . . . she'd raise herself, the poor girl, with my help, and have the medicine and look at me and my heart'd literally beat faster and faster. But all the while she was getting worse, worse and worse, and I thought she's bound to die, bound to. Believe me, I was ready to lie down in the coffin myself, what with the mother and the sisters seeing it all and looking me straight in the eyes, their confidence gradually slipping away: "What's wrong? How is she?" "Oh, it's nothing, nothing at all!" And how could it be nothing at all when her mind was already being affected? So there I am one night, sitting once again beside the sick girl. The maid's also there, snoring her head off . . . you couldn't blame her really, she'd been chivvied from pillar to post. Alexandra Andreyevna'd felt bad all evening; the fever'd tormented her. Right up until midnight she'd been tossing and turning and then she'd finally gone to sleep; or at least she lay there quietly. The lamp in the corner was burning before the icon and I sat there, you know, bent up, also snoozing. Suddenly, as if someone'd given me a shove in the side, I turned round and there – good God! – was Alexandra Andreyevna looking me straight in the eyes, with her lips apart and her cheeks literally on fire. "What's wrong?" "Doctor, I'm going to die, aren't I?" "God forbid!" "No, doctor, no, please, don't tell me I'll live . . . don't say that . . . Oh, if only you knew! . . . Listen, for God's sake don't hide from me what my condition is really!" She spoke, taking such quick breaths. "If I know for sure I'm going to die, then I'll tell you everything, everything!" "Please, Alexandra Andreyevna, please!" "Listen, I've not slept at all and I've been watching you . . . for God's sake . . . I trust you, you're a good man, you're an honest man, I beg you in the name of all that's holy, tell me the truth! If only you knew how important it is for me . . . Doctor, for God's sake tell me, am I in danger?" "What can I tell you, Alexandra Andreyevna? Please don't . . ." "For God's sake I implore you!" "I can't hide from you, Alexandra Andreyevna, that you *are* in danger, but God is merciful . . ." "I'll die, I'll die . . ." And she was literally overjoyed. Her face became so happy I was frightened. "Don't be frightened, don't be frightened, death doesn't worry me at all." She suddenly raised herself and leant on one elbow. "Now . . . well, now I can tell you that I'm grateful to you from the bottom of my heart, that you're a good, kind man and I love you . . ." I started at her like an idiot and I felt real fright, you know . . . "Do you hear what I'm saying, I love you . . ." "Alexandra Andreyevna, I'm not worth it!" "No, no, you don't understand me, you don't understand . . ." And suddenly she stretched out her arms and seized me by the head and kissed me. Believe you me, I almost cried out. I flung myself on to my knees and buried my head in the pillows. She fell silent, her fingers quivering in my hair. I could hear her crying. I began comforting her, trying to assure her – oh, I don't know what it was I said to her! I said: "You'll wake up the maid, Alexandra Andreyevna . . . Thank you, thank you, believe me . . . now be quiet." "That's enough of that, enough," she went on saying. "God be with them, let them all wake up, let them all come in here, I don't care, after all I'm going to die . . . What's wrong with you, why d'you look so scared? Lift your head up . . . Or maybe you don't love me, maybe I've made a mistake? . . . In that case forgive me." "Alexandra Andreyevna, what're you saying? . . . I love you, Alexandra Andreyevna." She looked me straight in the eyes and opened her arms. "Hold me, then." I'll tell you in all honesty I don't know how I didn't go mad that night. I felt that my sick girl was driving herself crazy. I could see she wasn't in her right mind and I realized that if she hadn't thought herself about to die she wouldn't have given me a single thought. You know, like it or not, it's horrible to be dying at twenty-five years of age without ever having loved someone – and that's what was driving her crazy, that's why, out of desperation, she'd chosen me . . . Do you see now what I mean? Well, she wouldn't let me out of her arms. "Have pity on me, Alexandra Andreyevna, and have pity on yourself," I said. "Why?" she said. "What's pity got to do with it? After all I'm going to die." She repeated this again and again. "If

15

I knew I'd be alive and again be a proper young lady, I'd be ashamed, really ashamed . . . but it's not like that, is it?" "But who said you're going to die?" "Oh, no, enough's enough, you can't fool me, you're a poor liar, you've only got to look at yourself to see that.' 'You will live, Alexandra Andreyevna, I'll cure you. We'll ask your mother's permission . . . and we'll get married and live happily ever after." "No, no, I've got your word for it, I've got to die . . . you promised me . . . you told me . . ." It was a bitter thing for me, bitter for many reasons. You know how it is, sometimes little things happen which seem nothing at all, but they hurt. It occurred to her to ask me my name, not my surname but my forename. As bad luck would have it, I'd been given the name Tripthong. Yes, yes, Tripthong, Tripthong Ivanych. In that household they all called me "doctor". There was nothing to be done about it, so I said: "Tripthong, milady." She screwed up her eyes, shook her head and whispered something in French – oh, something impolite – and then laughed, which was also bad. So that's how I spent practically the whole night with her. In the morning I left her room half out of my mind. I went back to her room in the afternoon, after tea. Oh, my God, oh, my God! I couldn't recognize her. I've seen better-looking corpses. In all honesty I swear to you I don't understand now, I really don't understand how I survived that torture. Three days and three nights my sick girl scraped by . . . and what nights! The things she said to me! And on the last night, just imagine, there I sat beside her and prayed to God that she'd be taken quickly, and me as well. Suddenly the old lady, her mother, came rushing in. I'd already told her, the mother, the day before that there was little hope, things were bad and it might be an idea to fetch the priest. The sick girl, on seeing her mother, said: "Oh, what a good thing you've come . . . Look at us, we love each other, we've given each other our word . . ." "Doctor, what's wrong, what's she saying?" I was stunned. "She's delirious," I said. "It's the fever." But she said: "Enough's enough, you were saying something quite different just now, and you accepted the ring from me . . . Why pretend now? My mother's kind, she'll forgive, she'll understand, and I'm dying, why should I tell a lie? Give me your hand . . ." I jumped up and ran out. The old lady, of course, guessed what'd happened.

'I won't weary you any longer, and in any case I find

17

it painful to remember. My sick patient died the following day. The Kingdom of Heaven be hers!' (The doctor added this rapidly and with a sigh.) 'Before she died she asked that the rest of the family should go and I should stay with her alone. "Forgive me," she said. "Perhaps I'm to blame in your eyes . . . it's the illness . . . but believe me, I never loved anyone more than you . . . don't forget me . . . take care of my ring . . ."'

The district doctor turned away. I took his hand.

'Oh,' he cried, 'let's talk about something else! Or perhaps you'd like a little game of whist? Chaps like us, you know, shouldn't give way to such highfalutin' feelings. Chaps like us should only bother with things like stopping the children crying or the wife scolding. Since then I've contracted a legal marriage, as they say . . . Well, you know . . . I found a merchant's daughter. Dowry of seven thousand roubles. She's called Akulina, which is about right for a Tripthong. She's a woman with a fierce tongue, but thankfully she's asleep all day . . . What d'you say to some whist?'

We sat down to whist for copeck stakes. Tripthong Ivanych won two and a half roubles off me and went home late, very content with his victory.

## Kasyan from the Beautiful Lands

I was returning from a hunting trip in a shaky little
cart and, under the oppressive effects of an overcast
summer day's stifling heat (it is notorious that on such
days the heat can be even more insufferable than on
clear days, especially when there is no wind), I was
dozing as I rocked to and fro, in gloomy patience,
allowing my skin to be eaten out by the fine white dust
which rose incessantly from beneath the heat-cracked
and juddering wheels on the hard earth track, when
suddenly my attention was aroused by the unusual
agitation and anxious body movements of my driver,
who until that instant had been in an even deeper doze
than I was. He pulled at the reins, fidgeted on his seat
and began shouting at the horses, all the time glancing
somewhere off to the side. I looked around. We were
driving through a broad, flat area of ploughed land
into which low hills, also ploughed up, ran down like

unusually gentle, rolling undulations. My gaze encompassed in all about three miles of open, deserted country; all that broke the almost straight line of the horizon were distant, small groves of birch trees with their rounded, tooth-shaped tips. Narrow paths stretched through the fields, dipped into hollows and wound over knolls, and on one of these, which was due to cross our track about five hundred yards from us, I could distinguish a procession. It was at this that my driver had been glancing.

It was a funeral. At the front, in a cart drawn only by one small horse, the priest was riding at walking pace; the deacon sat next to him and was driving; behind the cart, four peasants with bared heads were carrying the coffin, draped in a white cloth; two women were walking behind the coffin. The fragile, plaintive voice of one of the women suddenly reached my ears; I listened: she was singing a lament. Pitifully this ululant, monotonous and helplessly grieving melody floated in the emptiness of the fields. My driver whipped up the horses in the desire to forestall the procession. It is a bad omen to meet up with a corpse on the road. He did, in fact, succeed in galloping along the track just in time before the procession reached it.

But we had hardly gone a hundred yards farther on when our cart gave a severe lurch, keeled over and almost capsized. The driver stopped the wildly racing horses, leaned over from his seat to see what had happened, gave a wave of the hand and spat.

'What's wrong there?' I asked.

The driver got down without answering and with no sign of hurry.

'Well, what is it?'

'The axle's broken ... burned through,' he answered gloomily, and, in a sudden fit of temper, tugged so sharply at the breech-band of the trace-horse that the animal almost toppled over on her side. However, she regained her balance, snorted, shook her mane and proceeded with the utmost calmness to scratch the lower part of her front leg with her teeth.

I got down and stood for a short while on the road, resigning myself to a vague and unpleasant sense of bewilderment. The right wheel had almost completely turned inwards under the cart and seemed to lift its hub in the air in dumb resignation.

'What's to be done now?' I asked eventually.

'That's to blame!' said my driver, directing his whip towards the procession which by this time succeeded in turning on to the track and was beginning to approach us. 'I've always noticed it,' he continued. 'It's always a bad omen to meet up with a corpse, that's for sure.'

Again he took it out on the trace-horse who, seeing how irritable and severe he was, decided to stand stock-still and only occasionally gave a few modest flicks with her tail. I took a few steps to and fro along the track and stopped again in front of the wheel.

In the meantime, the procession had caught up with us. Turning aside from the track on to the grass, the sad cortège passed by our cart. My driver and I removed our caps, exchanged bows with the priest and looks with the pall-bearers. They progressed with difficulty, their broad chests heaving under the weight. Of the two women who walked behind the coffin, one was extremely old and pale of face; her motionless features, cruelly contorted with grief, preserved an expression of stern and solemn dignity. She walked in silence, now and then raising a frail hand to her thin, sunken lips. The other woman, of about twenty-five, had eyes that were red and moist with tears, and her whole face had become swollen from crying. As she drew level with us, she ceased her lament and covered her face with her sleeve. Then the procession went past us, turning back on to the track once more, and her piteous, heart-rending lament was resumed. After following with his eyes the regular to-and-fro motion of the coffin without uttering a sound, my driver turned to me.

'It's Martin, the carpenter, the one from Ryabovo, that they're taking to be buried,' he said.

'How do you know that?'

'I could tell from the women. The old one's his mother and the young one's his wife.'

'Had he been ill, then?'

'Aye . . . the fever . . . The manager sent for the doctor three days back, but the doctor wasn't home. He was a good carpenter, he was. Liked his drink a bit, but he was a real good carpenter. You see how his wife's grieving for him. It's like they say, though – a woman's tears don't cost nothin', they just flow like water, that's for sure.'

And he bent down, crawled under the rein of the trace-horse and seized hold of the shaft with both hands.

'Well,' I remarked, 'what can we do now?'

My driver first of all leaned his knees against the shoulder of the other horse and giving the shaft a couple of shakes, set the shaft-pad back in its place, crawled back once again under the rein of the trace-horse and, after giving her a shove on the nose while doing so, walked up to the wheel – walked up to it and, without taking his eyes off it, slowly extracted a snuff-box from beneath the skirt of his long tunic, slowly pulled open the lid by a little strap, slowly inserted two thick fingers (the tips of them could hardly fit into the snuff-box at once), kneaded the tobacco, wrinkled up his nose in readiness, gave several measured sniffs, accompanied at each inhalation of the snuff with prolonged snorting and grunting, and, after painfully screwing up and blinking his tear-filled eyes, settled into deep thoughtfulness.

'So, what do you think?' I asked when all this was over.

My driver carefully replaced the snuff-box in his pocket, brought his hat down over his brows without touching it, simply by a movement of his head, and climbed thoughtfully up on to the seat.

'Where are you off to?' I asked, not a little amazed.

'Please be seated,' he answered calmly and picked up the reins.

'But how are we going to go?'

'We'll go all right.'

'But the axle . . .'

'Please be seated.'

'But the axle's broken . . .'

'It's broken, yes, it's broken all right, but we'll make it to the new village – at walking pace, that is. It's over there to the right, beyond the wood, that's where the new village is, what they call the Yudin village.'

'But d'you think we'll get there?'

My driver did not even deign to answer me.

'I'd better go on foot,' I said.

'As you please . . .'

He waved his whip and the horses set off.

We did, in fact, reach the new village, even though the right front wheel hardly held in place and wobbled in a most unusual fashion. It almost flew off as we negotiated a small knoll, but my driver shouted at it angrily and we successfully descended the far slope.

Yudin village consisted of six small, low-roofed huts which had already begun to lean to one side or the other despite the fact that they had no doubt been put up quite recently, and not even all the yards had wattle fencing. As we entered the village, we did not meet a living soul; there were not even any chickens to be seen in the village street; there were not even

25

any dogs, save for one black, stubby-tailed animal that jumped hastily from a completely dried-up ditch, where it must have been driven by thirst, only to dash headlong under a gate without so much as giving a bark. I turned into the first hut, opened the porch door and called for the owners: no one answered me. I called again: a hungry miaowing came from behind the inner door. I shoved it with my foot and an emaciated cat flashed past me, its green eyes glittering in the dark. I stuck my head into the room and looked around: it was dark, smoky and empty. I went into the backyard and there was no one there. A calf gave a plaintive moo in the enclosure, and a crippled grey goose took a few waddling steps off to one side. I crossed to the second hut – and there was no one there either. So I went out into the backyard.

In the very middle of the brilliantly lit yard, right out in the middle of the sun, as they say, there was lying, face downward and with his head covered with a cloth coat, someone I took to be a boy. A few paces from him, beside a wretched little cart, a miserable little horse, all skin and bones, stood in a tattered harness under a straw overhang. Its thick reddish-brown coat was dappled with small bright splashes of sunlight that streamed through narrow openings in the dilapidated thatchwork. There also, high up in their little bird-houses, starlings chattered, looking down upon the world with placid inquisitiveness from their airy home. I walked up to the sleeping figure and began to rouse it.

The sleeper raised his head, saw me and at once jumped to his feet.

'What is it? What's happened?' he started muttering in bewilderment.

I did not answer him at once because I was so astonished by his appearance. Imagine, if you please, a dwarf of about fifty years old, with a small, swarthy, wrinkled face, a little pointed nose, barely discernible little brown eyes and abundant curly black hair which sat upon his tiny head just as broadly as the cap sits on the stalk of a mushroom. His entire body was extraordinarily frail and thin, and it is quite impossible to convey in words how unusual and strange was the look in his eyes.

'What is it?' he asked me again.

I explained the position to him and he listened to me without lowering his slowly blinking eyes.

'Is it not possible then for us to obtain a new axle?' I asked finally. 'I would gladly pay.'

'But who are you? Are you out hunting?' he asked, encompassing me with his glance from head to foot.

'I'm out hunting.'

'You shoot the birds of the air, eh? . . . And the wild animals of the forest? . . . Isn't it sinful you are to be killing God's own wee birds and spilling innocent blood?'

The strange little old man spoke with a very pronounced dwelling on each word. The sound of his voice also astonished me. Not only was there nothing decrepit about it but it was surprisingly sweet, youthful and almost feminine in its gentleness.

'I have no axle,' he added after a short interval of silence. 'This one won't do' – he pointed to his own little cart – 'because, after all, yours is a big cart.'

'But would it be possible to find one in the village?'

'What sort of village is it we have here! Here, there's not anyone of us has a single thing. And there's no one at home – aren't they all out at work for sure. Be off with you!' he said, suddenly, and lay down again on the ground.

I had certainly not expected an outcome of this kind.

'Listen, old man,' I started to say, touching him on the shoulder, 'have a heart, help me.'

'Be off with you in the name o' God! It's tired out I am, an' me having gone into town and back,' he told me and pulled his cloth coat over his head.

'Please do me a favour,' I went on, 'I . . . I'll pay you . . .'

'I'm not needin' your money.'

'Please, old man . . .'

He raised himself half-way and sat himself upright, crossing his delicate, spindly legs.

'It's takin' you I might be to where they've been cutting down the trees. 'Tis a place where some local merchants have bought a piece o' woodland, the Lord be the judge of 'em, an' they're getting rid of all the trees and putting up an office they are, the Lord judge 'em for it. That's where you might order an axle from 'em or buy one ready-made.'

'Excellent!' I exclaimed delightedly. 'Excellent! Let's go.'

'An oak axle, mind you, a good one,' he continued without rising from where he was sitting.

'Is it far to where they're cutting down the trees?'

'A couple o' miles.'

29

'Well, then, we can get there on your little cart.'

'Oh, but wait a moment . . .'

'Now come along,' I said. 'Come on, old man! My driver's waiting for us in the street.'

The old man got up reluctantly and followed me out into the street. My driver was in a thoroughly vexed state of mind: he had wanted to water the horses, but it had turned out that there was very little water in the well and what there was had an unpleasant taste; and that was putting first things first, as drivers are accustomed to say . . . However, as soon as he saw the old man he grinned broadly, nodded his head and cried out:

'If it's not little Kasyan! Good to see you!'

''Tis good to see you, Yerofey, righteous man that you are!' answered Kasyan in a despondent voice.

I at once told my driver about the old man's suggestion; Yerofey expressed his assent and drove into the yard. While Yerofey was quite deliberately making a great display of briskness in unharnessing the horses, the old man stood with one shoulder leaning against the gates and glanced unhappily either at him or me. He appeared to be at a loss and, so far as I could see, he was not unduly delighted by our sudden visit.

'Have they resettled you as well?' Yerofey suddenly asked him as he removed the shaft-bow.

'Me as well.'

'Yuck!' said my driver through his teeth. 'You know Martin, the carpenter . . . Martin of Ryabovo, don't you?'

'That I do.'

'Well, he's dead. We just met up with his coffin.'

Kasyan gave a shudder.

'Dead?' he muttered, and stared at the ground.

'Yes, he's dead. Why didn't you cure him, eh? People say you do cures, that you've got the power of healing.'

My driver was obviously taunting and making fun of the old man.

'And that's your cart, is it?' he added, shrugging a shoulder in its direction.

''Tis mine.'

'A cart, is it, a cart!' he repeated and, taking it by the shafts, almost turned it upside down. 'A cart, indeed! But what'll you be using to get to the clearings? You won't be able to harness our horse into those shafts. Our horses are big, but what's this meant to be?'

'I wouldn't be knowing,' answered Kasyan, 'what

you'll be using. For sure there's that poor creature,' he added with a sigh.

'D'you mean this?' asked Yerofey, seizing on what Kasyan had been saying, and, going up to Kasyan's miserable little horse, contemptuously stuck the third finger of his right hand in its neck. 'See,' he added reproachfully, 'gone to sleep, it has, the useless thing!'

I asked Yerofey to harness it up as quickly as possible. I wanted to go myself with Kasyan to the place where they were clearing the woodland, for those are the places where grouse are often found. When the little cart was finally ready, I somehow or other settled myself along with my dog on its warped, bast floor, and Kasyan, hunching himself up into a ball, also sat on the front support with the same despondent expression on his face – then it was that Yerofey approached me and, giving me a mysterious look, whispered:

'And it's a good thing, sir, that you're going with him. He's one of those holy men, you know, sir, and he's nicknamed The Flea. I don't know how you were able to understand him . . .'

I was about to comment to Yerofey that so far Kasyan had seemed to me to be a man of very good sense, but my driver at once continued in the same tone of voice:

'You just watch out and see that he takes you where he should. And make sure you yourself choose the axle, the stouter the better . . . What about it, Flea,' he added loudly, 'is there anywhere here to find a bite to eat?'

'Seek and it shall be found,' answered Kasyan, giving the reins a jerk, and we rolled away.

His little horse, to my genuine surprise, went far from badly. Throughout the entire journey Kasyan maintained a stubborn silence and answered all my questions peremptorily and unwillingly. We quickly reached the clearings, and once there we made our way to the office, a tall hut standing by itself above a small ravine which had been haphazardly dammed and turned into a pond. I found in this office two young clerks working for the merchants, both of them with teeth as white as snow, sugary sweet eyes, sugary sweet, boisterous chatter and sugary sweet, clever little smiles, did a deal with them for an axle and set off for the clearings. I thought that Kasyan would stay by the horse and wait, but he suddenly approached me.

'And is it that you're after shooting the wee birds?' he ventured. 'Is that it?'

'Yes, if I find them.'

'I'll go along with you. D'you mind?'

'Please do, please do.'

And we walked off. The area of felled trees extended for less than a mile. I confess that I looked at Kasyan more than at my dog. He had been aptly nicknamed the Flea. His black and hatless little head (his hair, by the way, was a substitute for any cap) bobbed up and down among the bushes. He walked with an extraordinarily sprightly step and literally took little jumps as he went, ceaselessly bending down, plucking herbs, stuffing them under his shirt, muttering words through his nose and shooting glances at me and my dog, giving us such keen and unusual looks. In the low bushes, the 'underbush' and in the clearings there are often little grey birds which all the time switch from sapling to sapling and emit short whistling sounds as they dive suddenly in their flight. Kasyan used to tease them, exchanging calls with them; a young quail would fly up shrilly from under his feet and he would call shrilly after it; a lark might start rising above him, fluttering its wings and pouring out its song – Kasyan would at once catch up its refrain. But to me he said not a word.

The weather was beautiful, still more beautiful than

it had been before; yet there was still no lessening of the heat. Across the clear sky drifted, with scarcely a movement, a few distant clouds, yellowish-white, the colour of a late snowfall in the spring, flat in shape and elongated like furled sails. Their feathered edges, light and wispy as cotton, altered slowly but obviously with each passing instant; they were as if melting, these clouds were, and they cast no shadow. For a long while Kasyan and I wandered through the clearings. Young shoots which had not yet succeeded in growing more than a couple of feet high spread their thin, smooth stems round the blackened and squat stumps of trees; round, spongy fungoid growths with grey edges, the kind which they boil down to make tinder, adhered to these tree-stumps; wild strawberries spread their wispy pink runners over them; mushrooms were also ensconced there in tight family clusters. One's feet were continually becoming entangled and caught by the tall grass, drenched in the sun's heat; in all directions one's eyes were dazzled by the sharp, metallic flashes of light from the young, reddish leaves on the saplings; everywhere in gay abundance appeared sky-blue clusters of vetch, the little golden chalices of buttercups, the partly mauve, partly yellow flowers of

35

St John and Mary daisies; here and there, beside overgrown tracks, in which the traces of cart-wheels were
marked by strips of short-stemmed red grass rose piles
of firewood, stacked in six-foot lengths and darkened
by the wind and rain; slight shadows extended from
them in slanting rectangles – otherwise there was no
shade of any kind. A light breeze sprang up occasionally and then died. It would blow suddenly straight
into one's face and caper around, as it were, setting
everything happily rustling, nodding and swaying
about, making the supple tips of the fern bow grace-
fully, so that one was delighted at it; but then it would
again fade away, and everything would once more be
still. Only the grasshoppers made a combined whir-
ring, as if infuriated – such an oppressive, unceasing,
insipid, dry sound. It was appropriate to the unabating,
midday heat, as if literally engendered by it, literally
summoned by it out of the sun-smelted earth.

Without coming across a single covey, we finally
reached some new clearings. Here, recently felled
aspens were stretched sadly on the ground, pressing
down both grass and undergrowth beneath their
weight; on some of them the leaves, still green but
already dead, hung feebly from the stiff branches; on

others they had already withered and curled up. A special, extraordinarily pleasant acrid scent came from the fresh, golden-white chips of wood which lay in heaps about the moistly bright tree-stumps. Far off, closer to the wood, there could be heard the faint clatter of axes and from time to time, solemnly and quietly, as if in the act of bowing and spreading out its arms, a curly-headed tree would fall.

For a long while I could find no game; finally, a landrail flew out of an extensive oak thicket which was completely overgrown with wormwood. I fired: the bird turned over in the air and fell. Hearing the shot, Kasyan quickly covered his face with his hand and remained stock-still until I had reloaded my gun and picked up the shot bird. Just as I was preparing to move farther on, he came up to the place where the bird had fallen, bent down to the grass which had been sprinkled with several drops of blood, gave a shake of the head and looked at me in fright. Afterwards I heard him whispering: 'A sin! 'Tis a sin, it is, a sin!'

Eventually the heat forced us to find shelter in the wood. I threw myself down beneath a tall hazel bush, above which a young and graceful maple had made a beautiful spread of its airy branches. Kasyan seated

37

himself on the thick end of a felled birch. I looked
at him. Leaves fluttered slightly high above, and their
liquid, greenish shadows glided calmly to and fro
over his puny figure, clad somehow or other in a dark
cloth coat, and over his small face. He did not raise
his head. Bored by his silence, I lay down on my back
and began admiringly to watch the peaceful play of
the entwined leaves against the high, clear sky. It is
a remarkably pleasant occupation, to lie on one's
back in a forest and look upwards! It seems that you
are looking into a bottomless sea, that it is stretching
out far and wide *below* you, that the trees are not rising from the earth but, as if they were the roots of
enormous plants, are descending or falling steeply
into those lucid, grassy waves, while the leaves on the
trees glimmer like emeralds or thicken into a
gold-tinted, almost jet-black greenery. Somewhere
high, high up, at the very end of a delicate branch, a
single leaf stands out motionless against a blue patch
of translucent sky, and, beside it, another sways,
resembling in its movements the ripplings upon the
surface of a fishing reach, as if the movement were
of its own making and not caused by the wind. Like
magical underwater islands, round white clouds

gently float into view and pass by, and then suddenly the whole of this sea, this radiant air, these branches and leaves suffused with sunlight, all of it suddenly begins to stream in the wind, shimmers with a fugitive brilliance, and a fresh, tremulous murmuration arises which is like the endless shallow splashing of oncoming ripples. You lie still and you go on watching: words cannot express the delight and quiet, and how sweet is the feeling that creeps over your heart. You go on watching, and that deep, clear azure brings a smile to your lips as innocent as the azure itself, as innocent as the clouds passing across it, and as if in company with them there passes through your mind a slow cavalcade of happy recollections, and it seems to you that all the while your gaze is travelling farther and farther away and drawing all of you with it into that calm, shining infinity, making it impossible for you to tear yourself away from those distant heights, from those distant depths . . .

'Master, eh, master!' Kasyan suddenly said in his resonant voice.

I raised myself up in surprise; until that moment he had hardly answered any of my questions and now he had suddenly started talking of his own accord.

'What do you want?' I asked.

'Why is it now that you should be killing that wee bird?' he began, looking me directly in the face.

'How do you mean: why? A landrail is a game bird. You can eat it.'

'No, it wasn't for that you were killing it, master. You won't be eating it! You were killing it for your own pleasure.'

'But surely you yourself are used to eating a goose or a chicken, for example, aren't you?'

'Such birds are ordained by God for man to eat, but a landrail – that's a bird of the free air, a forest bird. And he's not the only one; aren't there many of them, every kind of beast of the forest and of the field, and river creature, and creature of the marsh and meadow and the heights and the depths – and a sin it is to be killing such a one, it should be let to live on the earth until its natural end ... But for man there is another food laid down; another food and another drink; bread is God's gift to man, and the waters from the heavens, and the tame creatures handed down from our fathers of old.'

I looked at Kasyan in astonishment. His words flowed freely; he did not cast around for them, but spoke with quiet animation and a modest dignity, occasionally closing his eyes.

'So according to you it's also sinful to be killing fish?' I asked.

'A fish has cold blood,' he protested with certainty, 'it's a dumb creature. A fish doesn't know fear, doesn't know happiness: a fish is a creature without a tongue. A fish doesn't have feelings, it has no living blood in it . . . Blood,' he continued after a pause, 'blood is holy! Blood does not see the light of God's sun, blood is hidden from the light . . . And a great sin it is to show blood to the light of day, a great sin and cause to be fearful, oh, a great one it is!'

He gave a sigh and lowered his eyes. I must admit that I looked at the strange old man in complete amazement. His speech did not sound like the speech of a peasant: simple people did not talk like this, nor did ranters. This language, thoughtfully solemn and unusual as it was, I had never heard before.

'Tell me, please, Kasyan,' I began, without lowering my eyes from his slightly flushed face, 'what is your occupation?'

He did not answer my question immediately. His gaze shifted uneasily for a moment.

'I live as the Lord ordains I should,' he said eventually, 'but as for an occupation, no, I don't have an occupation of any kind. 'Tis a poor mentality I have, right from when I was small. I work so long as I can, but it's a poor worker I'm being. There's nothing for me to do! My health's gone and my hands're all foolish. In the springtime, though, I catch nightingales.'

'You catch nightingales? Then why were you talking about not touching the beast of the forest and the field and other creatures?'

'Not to be killing 'em, that's the point; death will take what's due to it. Now there's Martin the carpenter: he lived his life, Martin the carpenter did, and he didn't have long and he died; and now his wife's grieving over her husband and her little ones . . . It's not for man nor beast to get the better of death. Death doesn't come running, but you can't run away from it, neither; nor must you be helping it along. I don't kill the nightingales, Good Lord preserve us! I don't catch them to cause them pain, nor to put their lives in any peril, but for man's enjoyment, for his consolation and happiness.'

'Do you go into the Kursk region to catch them?'

'I go into Kursk and I go farther, depending how things are. I sleep in the swamplands, and also I sleep in the woodlands, and I sleep all alone in the fields and in the wild places: that's where snipe do their whistling, where you can hear the hares crying, where the drakes go hissing ... At eventide I take note where they are, and come morning I listen out for them, at dawn I spread my net over the bushes. There's a kind of nightingale sings real piteously, sweetly and piteously, it does ...'

'Do you sell them?'

'I give 'em away to good people.'

'What d'you do apart from this?'

'What do I do?'

'What keeps you busy?'

The old man was silent for a moment.

'Nothing keeps me busy. 'Tis a poor worker I am. But I understand how to read and write.'

'So you're literate?'

'I understand how to read and write. The Lord God helped me, and some kind people.'

'Are you a family man?'

'No, I've got no family.'

'Why's that? They've all died, have they?'

'No, it's just like it wasn't my task in life, that's all. Everything's according to the will of God, we all live

43

our lives according to the will of God; but a man's got to be righteous – that's what! That means he must live a fitting life in God's eyes.'

'And you haven't any relatives?'

'I have ... I have, yes.' The old man became confused.

'Tell me, please,' I began. 'I heard my driver asking you, so to speak, why you hadn't cured Martin the carpenter? Is it true you can heal people?'

'Your driver's a just man,' Kasyan answered me thoughtfully, 'but he's also not without sin. He says I have the power of healing. What power have I got! And who is there has such power? It all comes from God. But there ... there are herbs, there are flowers: they help, it's true. There's marigold, there's one, a kindly herb for curing human beings; there's the plantains, too; there's nothing to be ashamed of in talking about them – good clean herbs are of God's making. But others aren't. Maybe they help, but they're a sin and it's a sin to talk about them. Perhaps they might be used with the help of prayer ... Well, of course, there are special words ... But only he who has faith shall be saved,' he added, lowering his voice.

'Did you give anything to Martin?' I asked.

'I learned about him too late,' answered the old man. 'And what would've been the good! It is all ordained for man from his birth. He was not a dweller, was Martin the carpenter, not a dweller on this earth: and that's how it turned out. No, when a man's not ordained to live on this earth, the sweet sunlight doesn't warm him like it warms the others, and the produce of the earth profits him nothing, as if all the time he's being called away . . . Aye, God rest his soul!'

'Have you been resettled here among us for long?' I asked after a short silence.

Kasyan stirred.

'No, not long: 'bout four years. Under the old master we lived all the time where we were, but it was the custodians of the estate who resettled us. The old master we had was a meek soul, a humble man he was – God grant he enter the Kingdom of Heaven! But the custodians, of course, decided justly. It looks like this is how it was meant to be.'

'But where did you live before this?'

'We came from the Beautiful Lands.'

'Is that far from here?'

''Bout sixty miles.'

'Was it better there?'

'It was better . . . much better. The land's free and open there, with plenty of rivers, a real home for us; but here it's all enclosed and dried up. We've become orphans here. There where we were, on the Beautiful Lands, I mean, you'd go up a hill, you'd go up – and, Good Lord, what wouldn't you see from there? Eh? There'd be a river there, a meadow there and there a forest, and then there'd be a church, and again more meadows going far, far off, as far as anything. Just as far as far, that's how you'd go on looking and looking and wonderin' at it, that's for sure! As for here, true – the land's better: loamy soil it is, real good loam, so the peasants say. But so far as I'm concerned, there's sufficient food everywhere to keep me going.'

'But if you were to tell the truth, old fellow, you'd want to be where you were born, wouldn't you?'

'For sure I'd like to take a look at it. Still, it doesn't matter where I am. I'm not a family man, not tied to anywhere. And what would I be doing sittin' at home a lot? It's when I'm off on my way, off on my travels,' he began saying in a louder voice, 'that everything's surely easier. Then the sweet sunlight shines on you, and you're clearer to God, and you sing in better tune. Then you look-see what herbs is growing there, and

you take note of 'em and collect the ones you want.
Maybe there's water runnin' there, water from a
spring, so you have a drink of it and take note of that
as well. The birds of the air'll be singing . . . And then
on t'other side of Kursk there'll be the steppes, O
such steppelands, there's a wonder for you, a real joy
to mankind they are, such wide expanses, a sign of
God's bounty. And they go on and on, people do say,
right to the warm seas where Gamayun lives, the bird
of the sweet voice, to the place where no leaves fall
from the trees in winter, nor in the autumn neither,
and golden apples do grow on silver branches and
each man lives in contentment and justice with
another . . . That's where I'd like to be going . . .
Though I've been about a bit in my time! I've been
in Romyon and in Sinbirsk, that fine city, and in Mos-
cow herself, dressed in her golden crowns. And to
Oka, river of mother's milk, I've been, and to Tsna,
fair as a dove, and to our mother, the Volga, and
many's the people. I've seen, good Christians all, and
many's the honest towns I've been in . . . But I'd still
like to be going to that place . . . and that's it . . . and
soon-like . . . And it's not only I, sinner that I am, but
many other Chrestians that go walking and wandering

47

through the wide world with nothin' but bast on their feet and seekin' for the truth ... Sure they are! ... But as for what's at home, eh? There's no justice in the way men live – that's what ...'

Kasyan uttered these last words with great speed and almost inaudibly: afterwards he said something else, which I was unable even to hear, and his face took on such a strange expression that I was spontaneously reminded of the title 'holy man' which Yerofey had given him. He stared down at the ground, gave a phlegmy cough and appeared to collect his senses.

'O the sweet sun!' he uttered almost under his breath. 'O such a blessing, Good Lord! O such warmth here in the forest!'

He shrugged his shoulders, fell silent, glanced round distractedly and started singing in a quiet voice. I could not catch all the words of his protracted little song, but I heard the following words:

> But Kasyan's what they call me,
> And by nickname I'm the Flea ...

'Ha!' I thought, 'he's making it up ...'

Suddenly he shuddered and stopped his singing, gazing intently into the forest thicket. I turned and saw a little peasant girl of about eight years of age, dressed in a little blue coat, with a chequered handkerchief tied over her head and a small wattle basket on her bare, sunburnt arm. She had obviously not expected to come across us here at all; she had stumbled on us, as they say, and now stood stock-still on a shady patch of grass in a green thicket of nut trees, glancing fearfully at me out of her jet-black eyes. I had scarcely had time to notice her when she at once plunged out of sight behind a tree.

'Annushka! Annushka! Come here, don't be frightened,' the old man called to her in a gentle voice.

'I'm frightened,' a thin little voice answered.

'Don't be frightened, don't be frightened, come to me.'

Annushka silently left her hiding-place, quietly made her way round – her child's feet scarcely made any noise in the thick grass – and emerged from the thicket beside the old man. She was not a girl of about eight years of age, as it had seemed to me at first judging by her lack of inches, but of thirteen or fourteen. Her whole body was small and thin, but very well-made and supple, and her beautiful little face was strikingly similar to Kasyan's, although Kasyan

49

was no beauty. The same sharp features, the same unusual look, which was both cunning and trustful, meditative and penetrating, and exactly the same gestures . . . Kasyan took her in at a glance as she stood sideways to him.

'You've been out picking mushrooms, have you?' he asked.

'Yes,' she answered with a shy smile.

'Did you find many?'

'Yes.' (She directed a quick glance at him and again smiled.)

'Are there any white ones?'

'There are white ones as well.'

'Come on, show them . . .' (She lowered the basket from her arm and partly raised the broad dock leaf with which the mushrooms were covered.) 'Ah!' said Kasyan, bending over the basket, 'they're real beauties! That's really something, Annushka!'

'Is she your daughter, Kasyan?' I asked. (Annushka's face crimsoned faintly.)

'No, she's just a relative,' Kasyan said with pretended indifference. 'Well, Annushka, you be off,' he added at once, 'and God be with you! Watch where you go . . .'

'But why should she go on foot?' I interrupted. 'We could take her home in the cart.'

Annushka blushed red as a poppy, seized hold of the basket by its string handle and glanced at the old man in alarm.

'No, she'll walk home,' he objected in the same indifferent tone of voice. 'Why shouldn't she? She'll get home all right . . . Off with you now!'

Annushka walked off briskly into the forest. Kasyan followed her with his eyes, then looked down at the ground and grinned to himself. In this protracted grin, in the few words which he had spoken to Annushka and in the sound of his voice as he was talking to her there had been ineffable, passionate love and tenderness. He again glanced in the direction that she had gone, again smiled and, wiping his face, gave several nods of the head.

'Why did you send her away so soon?' I asked him. 'I would have bought some mushrooms from her . . .'

'You can buy them there at home whenever you like, it's no matter,' he answered, addressing me with the formal 'You' for the first time.

'She's very pretty, that girl of yours.'

'No . . . how so? . . . she's just as they come,' he

51

answered with apparent unwillingness, and from that very moment dropped back into his former taciturnity.

Seeing that all my efforts to make him start talking again were fruitless, I set off for the clearings. The heat had meanwhile dissipated a little; but my bad luck or, as they say in our parts, my 'nothing doing' continued the same and I returned to the village with no more than a single landrail and a new axle. As we were driving up to the yard, Kasyan suddenly turned to me.

'Master, sir,' he began, 'sure I'm the one you should blame, sure it was I who drove all the game away from you.'

'How so?'

'It's just something I know. There's that dog of yours, a good dog and trained to hunt, but he couldn't do anything. When you think of it, people are people, aren't they? Then there's this animal here, but what've they been able to make out of him?'

It would have been useless for me to start persuading Kasyan that it was impossible to 'cast a spell' over game and therefore I did not answer him. At that moment we turned in through the gates of the yard.

Annushka was not in the hut; she had already arrived and left behind her basket of mushrooms.

Yerofey fixed the new axle, having first subjected it to a severe and biased evaluation; and an hour later I drove away, leaving Kasyan a little money, which at first he did not wish to accept but which later, having thought about it and having held it in the palm of his hand, he placed inside the front of his shirt. During this whole hour he hardly uttered a single word; as previously, he stood leaning against the gates, made no response to my driver's reproachful remarks and was extremely cold to me in saying goodbye.

As soon as I had returned I had noticed that my Yerofey was once again sunk in gloom. And in fact he had found nothing edible in the village and the water for the horses had been of poor quality. So we drove out. With a dissatisfaction that expressed itself even in the nape of his neck, he sat on the box and dearly longed to strike up a conversation with me, but in anticipation of my initial question he limited himself to faint grumblings under his breath and edifying, occasionally caustic, speeches directed at the horses.

'A village!' he muttered. 'Call it a village! I asked for some *kvas* and they didn't even have any *kvas* . . . Good God! And as for water, it was simply muck!' (He spat loudly.) 'No cucumbers, no *kvas*, not a

53

bloody thing. As for you,' he added thunderously, turning to the right-hand horse, 'I know you, you dissemblin' female, you! You're a right one for pretendin', you are . . .' (And he struck her with the whip.) 'That horse has gone dead cunnin', she has, and before it was a nice, easy creature . . . Gee-up there, look-see about it.'

'Tell me, please, Yerofey,' I began, 'what sort of a person is that Kasyan?'

Yerofey did not reply immediately: in general he was thoughtful and slow in his ways, but I could guess at once that my question had cheered and calmed him.

'The Flea, you mean?' he said eventually, jerking at the reins. 'A strange and wonderful man he is, truly a holy man, and you'd not find another one like him all that quick. He's, so to speak, as like as like our grey horse there: he's got out of hand just the same . . . that's to say, he's got out of the way of workin'. Well, of course, he's no worker. Just keeps himself going, but still . . . For sure he's always been like that. To start with he used to be a carrier along with his uncles: there were three of 'em; but after a time, well, you know, he got bored and gave it up. Started living at home, he did, but couldn't feel settled – he's restless as a flea. Thanks be to God, it happened he had a kind master who didn't force him to work. So from that time on he's been wanderin' here, there and everywhere, like a roaming sheep. And God knows, he's remarkable enough, with his being silent as a tree-stump one moment and then talking away all of a sudden the next – and as for what he says, God alone knows what that is. Maybe you think it's his manner? It's not his manner, because he's too ungainly. But he sings well – a bit pompous-like, but not too bad really.'

'Is it true he has the power of healing?'

'A power of healing! What would he be doing with that? Just ordinary he is. But he did cure me of scrofula . . . A lot of good it does him! He's just as stupid as they come, he is,' he added, after a pause.

'Have you known him long?'

'Long enough. We were neighbours of his in Sychovka, on the Beautiful Lands.'

'And that girl we came across in the wood – Annushka – is she a blood relation of his?'

Yerofey glanced at me over his shoulder and bared his teeth in a wide grin.

'Huh . . . Yes, they're relations. She's an orphan, got no mother and nobody knows who her mother was. But it's likely she's related to him: she's the spittin' image of him . . . And she lives with him. A smart girl, she is, no denying that; and a good girl, and the old man, he dotes on her: she's a good girl. And likely he'll – you may not believe it – but likely he'll take it into his head to teach his Annushka readin' and writin'. You never know, it's just the sort of thing he'd start: he's as extrardin'ry as that, changeable-like he is, even untellable . . . Hey, hey, hey!' My driver suddenly interrupted himself and, bringing the horses to a stop, leaned over the side and started sniffing. 'Isn't there a smell of burning? There is an' all! These new axles'll be the end of me. It seemed I'd put enough grease on. I'll have to get some water. There's a little pond over there.'

And Yerofey got down slowly from the box, untied a bucket, walked to the pond and, when he returned, listened with considerable pleasure to the way the axle-hole hissed as it was suddenly doused with water. About six times in the course of seven or so miles he had to douse the overheated axle, and evening had long since fallen by the time we returned home.